Isla & Pickle

The Pony Party

Kate McLelland

Picture
Kelpies

One morning Isla and her best friend Pickle got an exciting invitation.

To: Isla and Pickle

You are invited to a Pony Party

for Rosie's birthday!

Where: the beach

When: next Saturday, 1-3 pm

Rosie and Belle xx

P.S. Please bring your riding gear

"Dad, please, please, please can I go to the party?" asked Isla. "Of course," said Dad, "but you haven't learned to ride yet, Isla, and the party is next Saturday."

"It can't be that hard to ride Pickle," said Isla confidently.
"I'll ask Farmer Jess to give you some lessons," said Dad,
with a worried look.

Before their first lesson began, Isla had to mount Pickle – which was a lot harder than it looked! She tried standing on a little ladder.

She thought about using her trampoline.

After lots of tries, they found a good way.

Now Isla and Pickle were ready to start walking.

"Remember your balance!" warned Farmer Jess. "Because if you don't, you will end up in a muddle . . .

or in a puddle!"

"Never mind, Isla. Let's try again."

Next Isla and Pickle had to learn how to stop.
Isla had no trouble telling Pickle what to do.

But Pickle had a little trouble doing what he was told.
"STOP, PICKLE!"

"Don't worry, Isla, practice makes progress," said Farmer Jess.
"Riding you is hard, Pickle," sighed Isla. "But you are still my
very best friend."

Soon it was the day of Rosie's party.
Dad took Isla and Pickle down to the beach.

The children rode their ponies along the beach. Isla tried very hard to stay balanced on Pickle in the water . . .

over the sand . . .

and even through a
flock of noisy seagulls.

But then Pickle smelled the
delicious party food, and . . .

"Pickle, you are absolutely not allowed to eat that birthday cake!" Isla told him.

And to everyone's surprise . . .

Pickle did as he was told!

"Good boy, Pickle," said Isla. "You are my very best friend, and my brilliant new riding pal." After everyone sang Happy Birthday to Rosie, Isla found Pickle some 'well-done' treats.